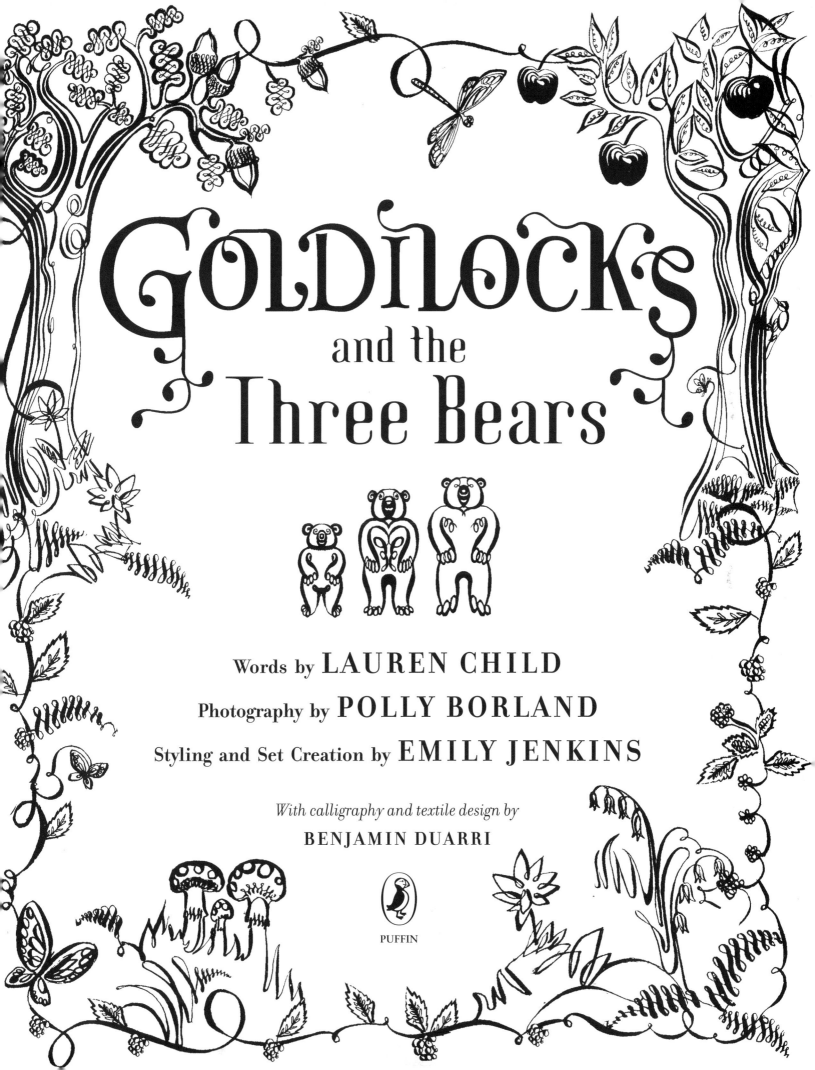

GOLDILOCKS
and the
Three Bears

Words by **LAUREN CHILD**

Photography by **POLLY BORLAND**

Styling and Set Creation by **EMILY JENKINS**

With calligraphy and textile design by
BENJAMIN DUARRI

PUFFIN

Once upon a time on the edge of a big dark forest, there lived a girl called Goldilocks. You've probably heard of her – if so, you will know these three things.

She was small

Her hair was all golden curls

And she looked like one of those very good children who never ever seem to get into trouble for anything . . .

Well the truth is, Goldilocks did get into trouble – quite a lot in fact – not because she was bad, but because her curiosity always got the better of her.

Now a little curiosity can be a wonderful thing, but too much and you have trouble.

And Goldilocks had a little more than too much.

Her mother often worried about letting Goldilocks out of her sight, but sometimes the little girl would ask just one too many questions and stick her fingers in one too many pots of honey and peek under the lid of one too many saucepans. And her mother, unable to bear it any longer, would send her out to collect firewood.

This was just such a morning and as Goldilocks slipped through the gate her mother called after her, "Remember these three things.

    Do not stray from the path

    Be back in time for breakfast

    And *whatever* you do – make *sure* you look after your little red shoes."

    "Oh I will, Mother," called Goldilocks. And she meant it – well, the bit about her little red shoes anyway.

OFF Goldilocks skipped, picking a flower here and looking down a rabbit hole there, lifting up pebbles and peering into tree trunks. But all the while she remembered her mother's words and she stuck to the path . . . well, at least until she saw a little blue bird pick up a snow-white feather and fly off into the trees.

"Oh," thought Goldilocks, "I wonder where he is going with that feather?" She couldn't help herself – and she ran through the forest after him.

So intent was she on following the bird that she didn't notice how far she had run, nor how thick the trees had become, until the bird was long gone and the path was well and truly lost.

Goldilocks stood all alone in the middle of the forest.

A LL Goldilocks could hear was the leaves rustling and the birds chirping and . . . well . . . *something* buzzing.

"I wonder who is making that noise," she thought. And she followed the buzzing until she came to a clearing where the sun shone down.

There, right in the middle of the trees, stood a curious wooden cottage and, next to it, three little wooden beehives, each of them surrounded by lots of buzzing bees.

"**H**OW STRANGE TO FIND a cottage right in the middle of the forest, I *wonder* why I have never seen this cottage before," thought Goldilocks, stretching up to peep in the tiny glass window.

She had to stand on tiptoe and even then she couldn't quite see, so she climbed up on to a flowerpot and her shoes got all muddy.

"Oh dear," said Goldilocks. "I said I would look after my little red shoes — perhaps whoever lives in this house would help me clean them."

So she knocked on the door. There was no answer, so she peeped through the keyhole.

"No one would mind if I had a look. *I* wouldn't mind if it were *my* house."

So she turned the handle and slipped inside.

"Hello," called out Goldilocks, "hello,
hello?" but no one answered and Goldilocks smiled
because she secretly hoped no one would be in.

"What a tidy little room," said Goldilocks out loud and,
as she said so, she bumped into a bucket of apples,
which tumbled on to the floor.

She didn't have a chance to pick them up because
something *rather* curious had caught her eye.

"How strange," she said, stepping over the apples,
"there seem to be three of everything.
There are one, two, three chairs
        and one, two, three bowls
        and one, two, three spoons
        and so one, two, three *people* must live
in this little house."

WELL, she was almost right. You see, the tiny cottage did not belong to one, two, three *people*, but surprisingly, if you don't already know it, one, two, three *bears*.

A large father bear

a middle-sized mother bear

and a small baby bear.

I know, it's strange to have bears living in a little wooden cottage, but this *is* a fairy tale and strange things happen in fairy tales.

Every morning the three bears liked to go for a little walk before breakfast – it really gave them an appetite and it also gave their porridge a chance to cool down – bears do *not* like to burn their tongues.

The bears never bothered to lock their front door because who would walk into a bear's house uninvited? Well, the answer is – someone who didn't know it was a bear's house.

THE porridge smelled **very** good and Goldilocks *was* feeling rather hungry, and she looked at the table and she looked at the door and she looked at the porridge.

"**One** little taste would not be so bad – they won't even notice, not a taste from this **large bowl**." And picking up the **biggest** spoon, she dipped it into the **biggest** bowl. "*Ouch*," said Goldilocks, "*too hot*."

"Maybe this **middle-sized bowl** might be nicer. *Oh no*," said Goldilocks, "*too cold*. How can **anyone** eat cold porridge?"

"Perhaps if I just tried this little smaller bowl – that might be better."

And it was – in fact it was *just* **right**. In fact it was **so** just right that she had **another** bite and **another**, until – oh dear – it was **all gone**.
   "*Oops*," said Goldilocks. "Well never mind, there are **two** *more* bowls. They can share, *I* would share if it were *my* porridge."

"Hmm," said Goldilocks, looking round the room, "I wouldn't mind a little sit down – I feel *rather* full."

"What a big chair – I would like to sit on that chair." But she didn't like it at all. "Too tall, too wobbly."

"Well, maybe I will sit on the middle-sized chair" – she sat down with a thud – "*Ouch, too low!*"

"Well, that small chair is sweet and more *my* size," said Goldilocks, as she sat down on the smallest chair. "Oh, this is *just* perfect for me."

But it wasn't and the chair broke into three pieces.

"Oh dear," said Goldilocks. "Well, it was an accident, I don't suppose anyone would mind if they knew it was an accident."

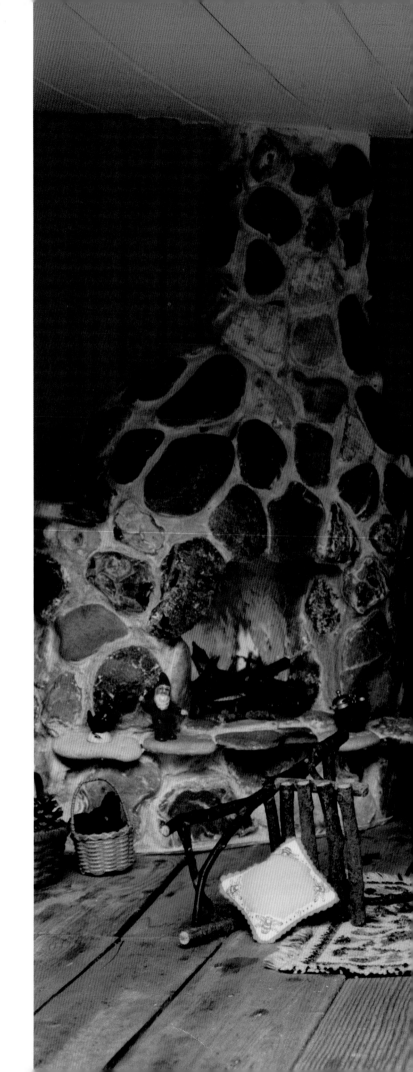

A S GOLDILOCKS PICKED HerSELF up off the floor, she caught sight of the twisty wooden stairs. "Stairs. I *wonder* why I didn't notice those before."

The answer is because she was too busy eating other people's porridge and breaking other people's furniture to have possibly noticed the little staircase winding up through the house.

"Now I *wonder* what is up there," she whispered.

Well, I think she knew very well what was up there – because most people do – but you see, Goldilocks just wanted to see for herself.

And so she climbed the stairs three at a time, snagging her stripy woollen stockings as she went.

I am sure you will not be surprised to hear that at the top of the stairs she
found a bedroom, and in that bedroom were three neatly made beds,
covered in three neat quilts, with three plump feather pillows.

"What a dear little room," she said, looking around. "If this were *my* house
I would sleep in that big bed."

But it wasn't as comfortable as it looked. "*Oh, too hard!*" complained Goldilocks.

You would think she would have learned by now.

"Well, maybe this **middle-sized bed** will be more **bouncy**."

And it was, but it was **too bouncy** and made her feel a little dizzy.

"*Hmm, too soft*. I suppose that little bed might be the one for me."

And as I am sure you have already guessed, it was.

"Oh yes, *just* **right**," said Goldilocks, slipping under the covers.

"I am so terribly, **terribly sleepy** – maybe I will lie down, just for **three** minutes. I'd better take my **shoes** off though," she said, noticing the mud that she had quite **forgotten** to clean off.

So Goldilocks carefully placed her little red shoes **neatly by the side of the** bed and fell soundly asleep.

WHEN the three bears came back from their walk they were very, very hungry.

They all sniffed the air – but it wasn't porridge they could smell. You see bears have very keen noses and right away they could sniff a *very* different smell.

Sniff

Sniff

Sniff

They looked around.

Father Bear noticed at once that something was quite wrong.

"Things are *not* as they should be," said Father Bear, picking up an apple.

FATHER BEAR WALKED OVER to the table and looked into his bowl. He picked up his spoon. "Who has been eating *my* porridge?"

"Hmm," said Mother Bear.
   "Who has been eating *my* porridge?"

"Oh," said Small Bear.
   "Who has been eating *my* porridge . . .
And look – they've gobbled it all up!"

A large tear welled up in Small Bear's eye and rolled down his little face. He was a sensitive type and also very fond of porridge.

FATHER Bear looked around to see if he could see where the *greedy* whoever-it-was might be, but what he saw was his chair – and he wasn't too pleased.

"Who has been sitting in *my* chair?"
Father Bear did *not* like people sitting in his chair.

Mother Bear looked at her chair and was not very pleased either.
"Who has been sitting in *my* chair?"

And Small Bear was the least pleased of them all because he no longer *even* had a chair.
"Who has been sitting in *my* chair . . .
And look, they have broken it all into pieces!"

MOTHER Bear looked around and what she saw was a thread of black wool winding up the stairs. "Things are *not* as they should be," said Mother Bear, picking up the end of the woollen thread.

The **three** bears started to climb the stairs.

Creak

Creak

Creak

But Goldilocks didn't stir, not *even* a lock of her golden hair, so soundly was she sleeping.

WHEN the bears got to the top of the stairs they listened carefully – bears have **very** sensitive ears – but all they could hear was a tiny, tiny sound almost like the sound of a sleeping mouse.

Father Bear looked at his bed. "Who has been sleeping in *my* bed?" he snarled.

Mother Bear looked at her bed – the quilt was all ruffled and the pillow unplumped. "Who has been sleeping in *my* bed?" she growled.

"Well," whispered Small Bear, "who has been sleeping in *my* bed?

And

by

the

way . . .

"...look, they are *still* here!"

And all three bears peered at the sleeping girl lying in Small Bear's bed.

Growl

Growl

Growl

And *exactly* then, Goldilocks woke from her slumber to see three differently sized bears staring down at her.

Now Goldilocks was a curious girl, but she wasn't curious enough to strike up a conversation with bears.

No, no, no!

GOLDILOCKS sprang from the bed and, as quick as quick, jumped out of the tiny open window – happily for her it wasn't **too big** a drop –

and she ran

and she ran

and she ran

as fast as she could, back to her cottage on the edge of the forest.

I can tell you her mother *wasn't* **too pleased** because she had missed breakfast – not that Goldilocks minded because she was still quite full with porridge. And she was *so* relieved to be home in **one** piece that she didn't *even* mind being sent to her room.

But she had forgotten **two** little things.

TWO
little
red shoes.

When her mother realised, she was extremely cross, as you might imagine. And Goldilocks was very sad because she **loved** her little red shoes. But Small Bear, well he was *very* happy indeed.

Mother Bear made him some more porridge, Father Bear mended his chair and Small Bear had an *almost* brand-new pair of little red shoes to wear when he went for his walk before breakfast.

And Small Bear
looked after them
very carefully indeed.

To Mary – L.C.

For Louie Moe Hillcoat – P.B.

For Martha – E.J.

Goldilocks and the Three Bears were specially designed and created by R. John Wright Dolls, Inc. USA
Doll and Bear design © R JOHN WRIGHT DOLLS, INC.
www.rjohnwright.com

Photographic development and printing supplied by Spectrum Photographic
With colour hand-printing by Paul Lowe
Special thanks to Klair, Andy, Tim, Kay, Zoe and Steve
www.spectrumphoto.co.uk

With special thanks to Tony Clark for the beautiful miniature paintings
on the walls of the Three Bears' Cottage

♡

Emily and Polly would like to thank the following people
for their help and support in making this book:

Noah Taylor for all sorts of invaluable contributions

John Hillcoat for never-ending support

Lucia Rosenwald, our brilliant placement student

Toby Jarvis for constructing and storing the house

Kai at Tapestry for his craft and skill

James Bannon and Lewis and Co. for supplying a studio space

Daniel Jenkins for building the beautiful beehives

Sophy and Lesley Jenkins for their fabulous needlework

Mandy Suhr and Goldy Broad for creative vision

Sadie Fredericks and Tim Keegan for strong backs and great patience

David Charles Warburton for kindly lending a lovely book to a stranger

Stanmer Park Nursery for assistance outdoors

♡

PUFFIN BOOKS
Published by the Penguin Group: London, New York, Australia, Canada, India, Ireland, New Zealand and South Africa
Penguin Books Ltd, Registered Offices: 80 Strand, London WC2R 0RL, England
puffinbooks.com   First published 2008
1 3 5 7 9 10 8 6 4 2
Thank you to Martin Grant for taking the photo of Louie Moe Hillcoat